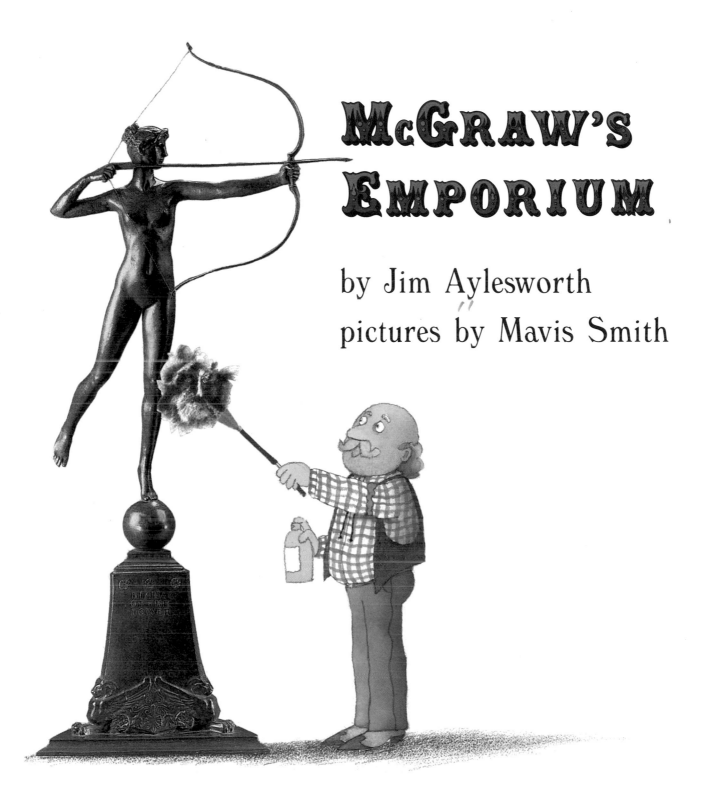

McGraw's Emporium

by Jim Aylesworth
pictures by Mavis Smith

Henry Holt and Company • New York

Henry Holt and Company, Inc.
Publishers since 1866
115 West 18th Street
New York, New York 10011

Henry Holt is a registered trademark of Henry Holt and Company, Inc.
Text copyright © 1995 by Jim Aylesworth
Illustrations copyright © 1995 by Mavis Smith. All rights reserved.
Published in Canada by Fitzhenry & Whiteside Ltd.,
195 Allstate Parkway, Markham, Ontario L3R 4T8.

Library of Congress Cataloging-in-Publication Data
Aylesworth, Jim. McGraw's Emporium / by Jim Aylesworth; pictures by Mavis Smith.
Summary: A boy searches for a gift for a sick friend at a unique
store, McGraw's Emporium, but finally settles on a free kitten.
[1. Sick—Fiction.   2. Stories, Retail—Fiction.   3. Gifts—
Fiction.   4. Stories in rhyme.]   I. Smith, Mavis, ill.   II. Title.
PZ8.3.A95Mc   1995   [E]—dc20   94-20486
ISBN 0-8050-3192-8
First Edition—1995
Printed in the United States of America on acid-free paper. ∞

1   3   5   7   9   10   8   6   4   2

The artist used watercolor, airbrush, colored pencil,
and collage to create the illustrations for this book.

To Akins and Aylesworth, Ltd.,
with love!

—J.A.

For my parents

—M.S.

My sweet young friend was sick in bed.
"I'll get him something nice!" I said.
A little gift to bring him cheer,
To chase the blues, and dry his tear.
But what to get that little guy?
I couldn't find a thing to buy!

Antiques

OPEN

And then, by chance, I passed a store
That had a sign hung by the door.
The sign read "Things from near and far.
Some things common, some quite bizarre."
And as I thought about that rhyme,
A man called, "Browse if you have time."

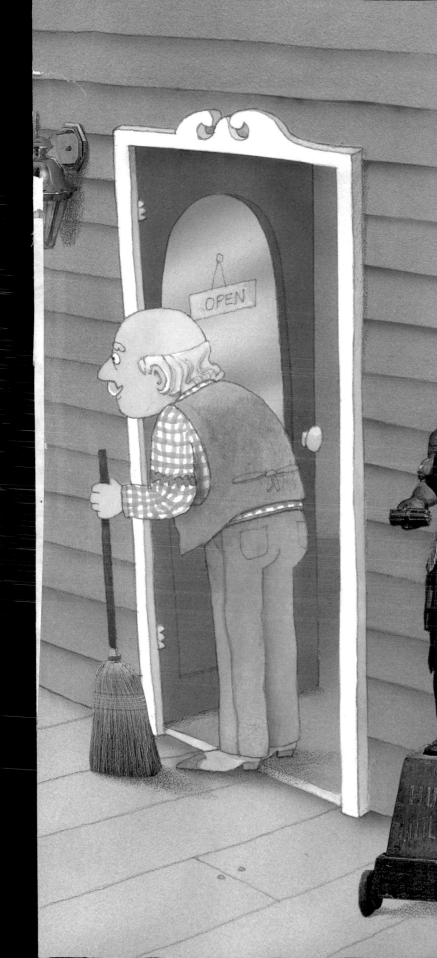

"Come in," he said. "Come take a peek."
"I'm sure to have just what you seek."
"Come in," he said. "My name's McGraw."
And once inside…the things I saw!

A cane, a clock, a feathered fan,

A vase, a bank, a frying pan,

A teddy bear, a bench, some shears,
A little stage for puppeteers,
A sword, a couch, a magazine,
A lamp that lights with kerosene,
A fishing rod, a pogo stick,
A book of hard arithmetic,
A valentine, a gong, a yoke,
A pitcher with its handle broke,

A low-cut gown of flowered lace,
A jug, a mug, a table base,
A rocking chair, three old TVs,
A pair of sailor's dungarees,

A checkered suit with wide lapels,
A box of pretty cockleshells,
A dress from China, shoes from Greece,
A phonograph, an old valise,
A chest of drawers, five roller skates,

A set of heavy iron weights,
A gum machine, a radio,
A cooker for the patio,

A Franklin stove, a cowboy hat,
A parrot cage, a cricket bat,
A little knife for spreading jam,
A sweater with a monogram,
A mandolin, nine picture frames,
A board for playing checker games,
A bowling ball, a kitchen sink,
A statue of King Tut, I think.

A garden hoe, a telescope,
A Scrabble game, a coil of rope,
A model ship, a baby's crib,
A record by the Brothers Gibb,
A Barbie doll with no left shoe,
A totem pole, a billiard cue,
A rhinestone ring, a coffeepot,
A bongo drum, an army cot,
A pair of socks for keeping warm,

A royal captain's uniform,
A hockey puck, an arrowhead,
A saddle for a Thoroughbred,
A bracelet with lots of charms,
A mannequin without her arms,
A Frisbee disk, a wheel, a buoy,
A license plate from Illinois,

A chandelier, an oar, a gate,
A calendar from 'forty-eight,
A canvas tent, a gerbil home,
A cooler made of Styrofoam,
A figurine, a wrench, a stool,
A carpet made in Istanbul,
A blondish wig, a clarinette,
A counter from a luncheonette,

A lantern from an old caboose,
A tool for making orange juice,
A rack for coats, a plaster swan,
A pillow from Saskatchewan,

A rubber duck, a pair of skis,
A megaphone, a hive for bees,
A map of France, a laundry press,
A thing for milking cows, I guess.

A metronome, a silver spoon,
A boxing glove, a brass spittoon,
A target for a game of darts,
A puzzle missing several parts,
A ladder with a broken rung,
A cello with its strings unstrung,
A rolltop desk, a quilt, a D,

A shirt from sunny Waikiki,

A pedestal, a baby grand,
A red coat from a marching band,
A mortarboard, a Union Jack,
A hubcap off a Pontiac,
A camera, a blunderbuss,
A coconut, an abacus,
A scarf, a harp, a mask, a bell,
A horsey from a carousel,
A boomerang, an hourglass,
A lance once used at Khyber Pass,
A samovar, a bone, a stein,
A bust of George, a traffic sign,

A blanket made of tartan plaid,
A muff that someone's gramma had,
A spatula, a mounted fish,
A bike, a scale, a candy dish,
A globe, a robe, some winter boots,
A loving cup, some plastic fruits,
A purse, two ties, a fake fur coat,
A banner that says "Go and Vote,"
A mustache cup, a powder puff,

And lots and lots of other stuff.

'Twas then I saw, pinned to the wall,
A note that read
"Free kittens!
Call!"
"The perfect gift!" I cried. "At last!"
I copied down the number fast.

FREE
KITTENS
CALL
555-CATS

"McGraw," I said, "I love your store,
But I can't stay one minute more."
I shook his hand and said, "Good day!"
Went out the door, and on my way.